"All in a Night's Work"

So says Sheriff John after a bizarre night in which he single-handedly put a stop to a drunken brawl at the saloon, caught a gang of four robbers at the Sunshine Bank, rounded up cattle rustlers at Clayton McDermott's ranch, and prevented a range war from breaking out.

Trouble began at the Long Horn Saloon around nine o'clock last night when Ewen Clemm lost his week's wages at a poker game. Clemm began a fight that quickly turned into a brawl. Sheriff John was summoned and quickly restored order to the drinking establishment.

At the same time, across the street, robbers had broken into the Sunshine Bank and were about to break into the safe, when Sheriff John showed up and caught them red handed. The bank manager M. P. Cunius made no comments this morning other than to say that the money was all there, thanks to Sheriff John.

No sooner had Sheriff John left the bank than he headed out to Clayton McDermott's ranch, some five miles south of town, where he lassoed and hogtied two rustlers about to make off with McDermott's prize longhorn steer.

As if that were not enough for our hero, the cattlemen and the sheep herders threatened to start a range war, the likes of which had never been seen in these parts. Sheriff John calmed the situation and made both sides agree to come into town and talk things out.

But, by far, the most curious turn of events, folks say, was that Sheriff John was able to restore law and order to our town without wearing his famous hat.

Asked about this and last night's troubles, Sheriff John made this comment, "Well, boys, all I have to say is: it's not your hat, it's your heart."

Married on August 4th—Sheriff John to Miss Lil, at the Sunshine Chapel.

THIS IS A BORZOI BOOK PUBLISHED BY ALFRED A. KNOPF

Text and illustrations copyright © 2007 by James Rumford

Published in the United States by Alfred A. Knopf, an imprint of Random House
Children's Books, a division of Random House, Inc., New York.

KNOPF, BORZOI BOOKS, and the colophon are registered trademarks of Random House, Inc.

www.randomhouse.com/kids

Educators and librarians, for a variety of teaching tools, visit us at
www.randomhouse.com/teachers

Library of Congress Cataloging-in-Publication Data
Rumford, James.
Don't touch my hat! / by James Rumford. — 1st ed.
p. cm.
SUMMARY: A sheriff in the Old West fights crime with the help of his lucky ten-gallon hat.
ISBN 978-0-375-83782-1 (trade)
ISBN 978-0-375-93782-8 (lib. bdg.)
[1. Hats—Fiction. 2. Luck—Fiction. 3. Superstition—Fiction. 4. West (U.S.)—Fiction.]
I. Title. II. Title: Do not touch my hat!.
PZ7.R8878Do 2007
[E]—dc22
2006003682

The illustrations in this book were inspired by early-twentieth-century movie posters,
pulp fiction covers, and the ingenious art of Leonetto Cappiello (1875–1942).

MANUFACTURED IN MALAYSIA

February 2007
10 9 8 7 6 5 4 3 2 1

First Edition

To hat lovers everywhere
and the kids at
Waipahu Elementary School

DON'T TOUCH MY HAT!

James Rumford

Alfred A. Knopf   New York

Out West, a lonesome prairie or two from anywhere, was a town called Sunshine.

Sunshine was smaller'n most,
bigger'n some, but cleaner and
more civ'lized than 'em all.
Sheriff John saw to that—
him and his ten-gallon hat.

Why, with that hat on, he could round up rustlers, stop saloon fights, and deliver ladies in distress.

Bank robbers, train robbers, stagecoach robbers, any kinda robbers didn't have a chance 'gainst Sheriff John and his ten-gallon hat.

Without that sweat-stiff, trail-dusted, bullet-riddled hat, Sheriff John could do nothing—or so he thought.

So, when he was at the barber's, it was:

"FELLERS, DON'T TOUCH MY HAT!"

Takin' his Saturday bath:

"SUGAR, DON'T TOUCH MY HAT!"

Afore he turned out the light:

"NOW, DARLIN', DON'T TOUCH MY HAT!"

His wife, Lil,
late of the Longhorn Saloon,
felt jist a little put out.
"Why, he thinks more of that hat than
he does of me!"
'Course, she wasn't one to be shy
'bout hats neither. She had 'em all—
red ones, feathered ones, veiled ones,
hats made of straw or velvet, plain
beaver or fancy varmint.

And yesterday, to top it all,
she came a-prancin' home
with the fanciest one yet.

And so, on a quiet western night—moonless
and coyote-less—Sheriff John and Lil had
just turned down the light when . . .
the Ol' West went completely wild!

Rustlers were at
McDermott's ranch, robbers in
the bank. There was a fight at the saloon
and a range war a-brewin'.

"Sheriff!" yelled Deputy Bob. "Sheriff!
Come quick! There's trouble aplenty!"

No time for lantern lightin'. Sheriff
John pulled on his pants, jumped into
his boots, strapped on his gun. . . .

"I'm a-comin', Bob.
JIST LET ME
GIT MY HAT!"

"Darlin' sugar!" wailed Lil,
half hangin' out of the upstairs
window. But it was too late.
Sheriff John and Deputy Bob
were long gone.

Sheriff John put a stop to the fight.

He caught the robbers at the safe,

rounded up the rustlers,

and made peace
betwixt the sheep herders
and the cattlemen.

All before sunup,
thanks to his trusty ten-gallon hat.
But when he got back home,
Lil was a-waitin' for him. Let's just say
that Sheriff John had a lot of rethinkin'
to do, best summed up by this:

IT'S YOUR HEART, NOT YOUR HAT.

"Sorry, darlin', I ruint your new hat."

"Sugar, I'm jist glad you're home safe and sound."

THE END

E
Rum   Rumford, James
AUTHOR

TITLE   Don't Touch My Hat!

DATE	BORROWER'S NAME	DATE RETURNED

E   Don't Touch
Rum   my Hat!

Sheriff John Leaves Sunshine

Daily Sunshine Reporter
Winston I. Wright

It was a tearful goodbye yesterday when Sheriff John and his wife Lil boarded the train for California. After forty years as the town sheriff and friend to all who knew him, Sheriff John will be greatly missed.

A delicious dinner at the Sunshine Cafe was given in his honor and a plaque was presented to Sheriff John with the words "It's not your hat, it's your heart. We will miss you. The Town of Sunshine."

Sheriff John has been asked by Ponymount Pictures of Hollywood, California, to be a consultant to the stars for their newest cowboy talking pictures.

When asked about taking up a career so late in life, Sheriff John said, "Well sir, it's never too late to try something new. Besides someone has to show those Hollywood folks what the Old West was really like."

Hollywood HOOT

by Hervé Hodge

Well, the Academy Awards at the Coconut Grove are over, the Oscars taken home, and the glitter gone—until next year.

Even so, while lingering over my coffee at the Grove, I'd like to take a moment to present my own awards to those attending Hollywood's finest event.

The top award for best-dressed man, no question about it, goes to the one known about town as "Sheriff John" for his magnificent cowboy outfit topped off by the biggest ten-gallon hat anyone anywhere has ever seen.

Of course, not to be outdone by her husband, was Sheriff John's beautiful wife Lil, who wore a yellow-sequinned gown and a fabulous feathered hat designed by Claire Chenille. To her I give the award for best dressed woman.

Next comes my award for best smile throughout the entire evening of tears of joy and tears of disappointment. This award goes